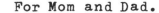

For Mom and Dad.
Thank you for daily stories, trips to the library,
and your never-ending support...even when I
wanted to be a five-foot-three Rockette.

—S.F.

As my oldest son, Magnus, says, "The trick to draw
well is pizza. If you eat a lot of pizza, you draw
well...." Hopefully this time I ate enough pizza.
To Tina, Magnus, and Nils.

—S.K.

For my wild bunch——Rachel, Samuel, and Matthew.

—G.M.

Designed by Tony Fejeran

Printed in the United States of America

First Hardcover Edition, January 2016

1 3 5 7 9 10 8 6 4 2

ISBN 978-1-4847-2102-5

FAC-03427-15338

Library of Congress Control Number: 2015947449

Visit www.disneybooks.com

Disney
ZOOTOPIA
JUDY HOPPS
AND THE MISSING
JUMBO-POP

By **SUZANNE FRANCIS**

Illustrated by **STÉPHANE KARDOS** and **GEORGE McCLEMENTS**

Disney PRESS
Los Angeles • New York

BEEP! BEEP! BEEP!

Judy SPRINGS out of bed and turns off her alarm clock.

BEEP! BEEP!

She is ready to
TAKE ON THE DAY

and make
THE WORLD

a *BETTER PLACE.*

RING! RING! This time it's Judy's phone. Her family is calling from Bunnyburrow . . .

On Judy's way to work, the subway is crowded with animals on their morning commutes. Judy smiles at them all—even grouchy George Lionel, who complains and complains.
Judy hops off at her stop:

the
ZOOTOPIA
POLICE
DEPARTMENT.

"Officer Hopps
reporting for duty!"

"Saved you a carrot doughnut," says Clawhauser. "Unless you don't want it. Can I have it?"

"It's yours," Judy says, and heads to her car so she can protect the city.

It's a busy day on the street. Carson's and Spencer's tempers have stopped traffic. With so many siblings, Judy is used to settling squabbles.

Suddenly, Judy hears a cry **FOR HELP.**

Ernie has lost his Jumbo-pop.
Officer Hopps is on the case!

"Where did you last see your **Jumbo-pop?**"

"In **Tundratown.**"

Ernie jumps into Officer
Hopps's car, and they head
to Central Station.

ZOOM! ZOOM!

At the station, Judy's coins clink into the meter. The fastest way to Tundratown is by train.

THEY HAVE

ONE HOUR

to find that pop before their meter expires!

"Tickets, please," says the conductor as he punches a hole in each one.

Ernie watches the circles of paper fly like confetti.

At Sahara Square, Ernie whispers, "I saw my uncle over there." He points to the Naturalist Club. "I wish he had been wearing pants!"

"Do you remember anything about the pop?" Judy asks. Ernie closes his eyes and thinks hard.

"Not yet."

They get off the train in Tundratown. Ernie remembers something when he sees his friend Amos. "We watched a hockey game. One of the reindeer took a slap shot, and the puck knocked Amos's loose tooth out!"

"Then you thaid you wanted a pop," Amos says, showing off his gaping smile.

"Oh, yeahhh," says Ernie.

"I went to Jumbeaux's Cafe!"

Inside Jumbeaux's the clerk remembers
Ernie. "You were looking for a Jumbo-pop that
was a special shade of red," the clerk says.
One of the customers remembers Ernie, too.
"You said you were going on a ride next."

"Right! On the gondola!"

Ernie says excitedly.

Get Your
Jumbo-pop
Here!

High above the city, Ernie feels hopeful. "My pop must be down there."

"We're going to find it," says Judy.

She notices her hand is sticky. "Red Jumbo-pop drippings," she says. "You definitely ate it in here."

"My pop," says Ernie.

"We're close to **solving this mystery,**"
says Judy.

"I remember!" Ernie blurts out. "After the gondola, I went to the museum!"

Back on the train they see someone with a tasty red Jumbo-pop.

"That looks just like mine!" says Ernie.

Judy investigates. Nope. It's Mayor Lionheart
with his little niece, Dandy. That's her Jumbo-pop.

"Aw, **peanuts,**" Ernie says.

At the Natural History Museum, Judy turns to Ernie. "How did you get in with the pop?" she asks. Then she sees the guard—sleeping. "Oh."

All of a sudden, Judy spies the corner of a ticket in Ernie's pocket. It's for the photo booth.

She puts the ticket in the booth, and out pop some very interesting pictures.

"You ate the pop, Ernie."

"Oh, yeah," he says. "And it was good! Mom says I can be a little forgetful."

Judy smiles and pats his head. Another case solved!

Meanwhile, in Little Rodentia, workers are building a new apartment building.

"Found this one over at the museum. Perfect shade of red, right?" asks a worker, holding up a stick.

Judy drives by in her police car and smiles.

Lights ignite and sparkle as the
city of Zootopia drifts off to sleep.
Judy hops into bed knowing
tomorrow will be another busy day
full of

MYSTERY,
ADVENTURE,
and
PEOPLE WHO NEED HER!